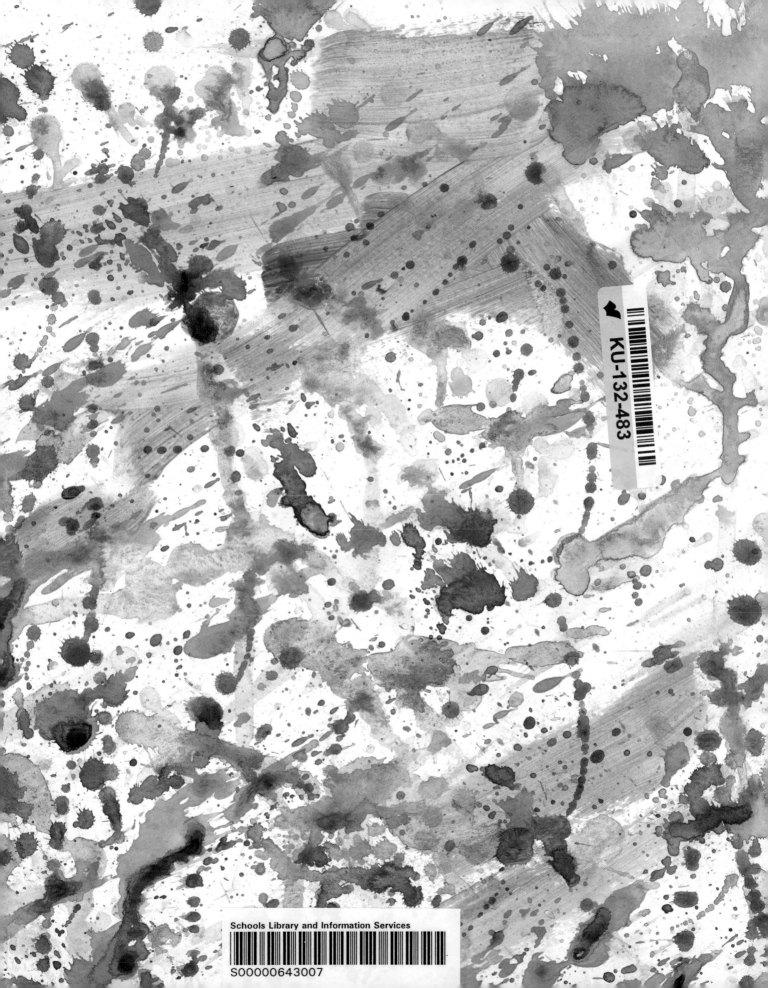

for Finn

Text and illustrations © by Ruth Brown, 2002
The rights of Ruth Brown to be identified as the author and illustrator of this work
have been asserted by her in accordance with the Copyright, Designs and Patents Act, 1988.
First published in Great Britain in 2002 by Andersen Press Ltd., 20 Vauxhall Bridge Road,
London SW1V 2SA. Published in Australia by Random House Australia Pty.,
20 Alfred Street, Milsons Point, Sydney, NSW 2061. All rights reserved.
Colour separated in Switzerland by Photolitho AG, Zürich.
Printed and bound in Italy by Grafiche AZ, Verona.

10   9   8   7   6   5   4   3   2   1

British Library Cataloguing in Publication Data available.

ISBN 1 84270 111 8

This book has been printed on acid-free paper

Helpful Henry

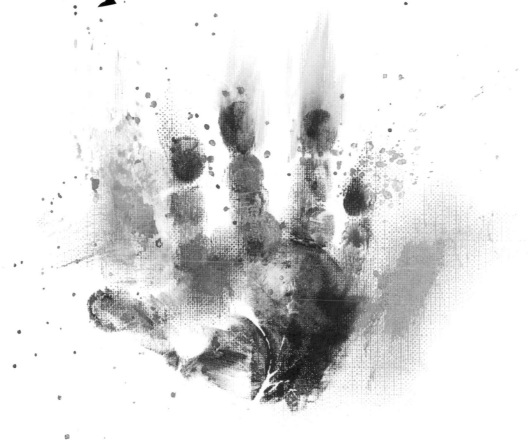

written and illustrated by
Ruth Brown

Andersen Press
London

Henry was a helpful lad.
He thought he'd make his mother glad
By polishing the bathroom floor,

Then the mirror and the door.

He cleaned around the taps and plug,

And the rubbish bin and rug.

The basin, toilet bowl and tub
All received a special scrub.

"That's Daddy's facecloth!"
Mother screamed.
"I'm only helping,"
Henry beamed.

In the morning when he woke,
Henry put his socks in soak.
Washing all the clothes he had
Was bound to please his mum
and dad.

Then he washed his boots and hat,

Then the cushions,

and the cat.

The sink was full. The water flowed
Through the doorway, down the road.

Mum and Dad thought it was rain,
Until they saw the soap-filled drain.

"You've caused a flood!"
his parents cried.

"I'm only helping,"
Henry sighed.

Dad had worked so very hard,
Painting, outside in the yard.

Henry liked the colour blue,
So thought he'd do some painting, too.

He liked the colour such a lot,
He painted both his chair and cot.

He painted round the
window frame,

And his cupboard, just the same.

He did the door and handle, too,
In his favourite colour – blue!

"What a mess," his father grumbled.
"I was *helping*," Henry mumbled.

One day, Henry thought he'd make
His mum and dad a special cake.

He mixed some butter,
eggs and salt,

Cornflakes, flour,
milk and malt.

Then he thought it would be nice
Just to add some herbs and spice.

Some sugar next, and then some cheese,
Carrots, apples, beans and peas –

All were added to the tin,
And very carefully mixed in.

But when his mother saw the mess
She cried aloud in deep distress.
She rolled her eyes
and banged her head.
"I'm only helping,"
Henry said.

But change was coming Henry's way,
For on one sunny autumn day
His father said it was the rule
That every child must go to school.

"You'll learn to read and write and spell –
And draw and dance and play as well.
With lots of kids it's much more fun
Than being just the only one."

But Henry wasn't quite so sure,
When they reached the large school door.
He kissed his mum and dad goodbye,
And thought he was about to cry.
So, to make himself feel brave,
He turned and gave a cheery wave.

Everything was strange and new.
Henry wondered what to do . . .

Everyone at first felt shy,
But later on, as time went by,
They all began to settle in
And the school day could begin.

First of all, they made some pies.
Then, to Teacher's great surprise –

Henry quickly cleaned the sink,
And handed out the juice to drink!

He washed the brushes, one by one,
When all the paintings had been done.

He re-arranged the box of books,

And hung the coats back on the hooks.

He'd filled the sand-tray up, as well,
When suddenly he heard the bell.

Henry was surprised how fast
His very first whole school day passed!

Henry's mum had said she'd wait
To pick him up, by the gate.

Children tumbled out the door
Every minute, more and more.

Then, last of all, came Henry and
The teacher led him by the hand
Towards his mother, now alone:

"Oh no," she groaned. "What's Henry done?"

But Teacher laughed
and said, "I'm sure
That I have NEVER met before
Such a very helpful child."

Henry looked at Mum
and smiled.

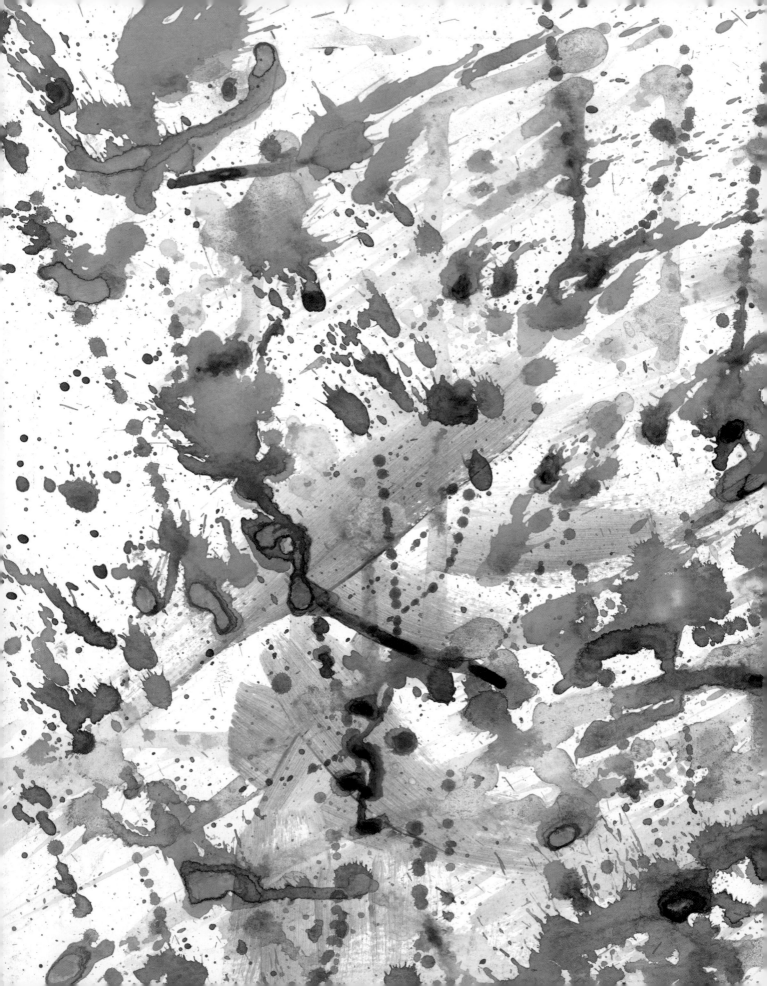